The Embassy
of Cambodia

ZADIE SMITH

HAMISH HAMILTON
an imprint of
PENGUIN BOOKS

HAMISH HAMILTON

Published by the Penguin Group

Penguin Books Ltd, 80 Strand, London WC2R 0RL, England

Penguin Group (USA) Inc., 375 Hudson Street, New York, New York 10014, USA

Penguin Group (Canada), 90 Eglinton Avenue East, Suite 700, Toronto, Ontario,
Canada M4P 2Y3 (a division of Pearson Penguin Canada Inc.)

Penguin Ireland, 25 St Stephen's Green, Dublin 2, Ireland (a division of Penguin Books Ltd)

Penguin Group (Australia), 707 Collins Street, Melbourne, Victoria 3008, Australia
(a division of Pearson Australia Group Pty Ltd)

Penguin Books India Pvt Ltd, 11 Community Centre, Panchsheel Park, New Delhi – 110 017, India

Penguin Group (NZ), 67 Apollo Drive, Rosedale, Auckland 0632, New Zealand
(a division of Pearson New Zealand Ltd)

Penguin Books (South Africa) (Pty) Ltd, Block D, Rosebank Office Park,
181 Jan Smuts Avenue, Parktown North, Gauteng 2193, South Africa

Penguin Books Ltd, Registered Offices: 80 Strand, London WC2R 0RL, England

www.penguin.com

First published in the USA in the *New Yorker* 2013
Published in Great Britain by Hamish Hamilton 2013

001

Copyright © Zadie Smith, 2013

The moral right of the author has been asserted

Set in 11.75/18.25pt Fournier MT Std
Typeset by Jouve (UK), Milton Keynes
Printed in Great Britain by Clays Ltd, St Ives plc

A CIP catalogue record for this book is available from the British Library

ISBN: 978–0–241–14652–1

www.greenpenguin.co.uk

O—I

Who would expect the Embassy of Cambodia?
Nobody. Nobody could have expected it, or be
expecting it. It's a surprise, to us all. The Embassy
of Cambodia!

Next door to the embassy is a health centre.
On the other side, a row of private residences,
most of them belonging to wealthy Arabs (or so
we, the people of Willesden, contend). They tend
to have Corinthian pillars on either side of their
front doors, and – it's widely believed – swimming
pools out the back. The embassy, by contrast, is
not very grand. It is only a four- or five-bedroom

north London suburban villa, built at some point in the 1930s, surrounded by a red-brick wall, about eight feet high. And back and forth, cresting this wall horizontally, flies a shuttlecock. They are playing badminton in the Embassy of Cambodia. Pock, smash. Pock, smash.

The only real sign that the embassy is an embassy at all is the little brass plaque on the door (which reads: 'THE EMBASSY OF CAMBODIA') and the national flag of Cambodia (we assume that's what it is – what else could it be?) flying from the red-tiled roof. Some say, 'Oh, but it has a high wall around it, and this is what signifies that it is not a private residence, like the other houses on the street, but rather an embassy.' The people who say so are foolish. Many of the private houses have high walls, quite as high as the Embassy of Cambodia – but they are not embassies.

O—2

On 6 August, Fatou walked past the embassy for the first time, on her way to a swimming pool. It is a large pool, although not quite Olympic size. To swim a mile you must complete eighty-two lengths, which, in its very tedium, often feels as much a mental exercise as a physical one. The water is kept unusually warm, to please the majority of people who patronize the health centre, the kind who come not so much to swim as to lounge poolside or rest their bodies in the sauna. Fatou has swum here five or six times now, and she is often the youngest person in the pool by several decades. Generally, the clientele are white, or else South Asian or from the Middle East, but now and then Fatou finds herself in the water with fellow Africans. When she spots these big men, paddling frantically like babies, struggling simply to stay afloat, she prides herself on her own abilities, having taught herself to swim, several years earlier, at the Carib Beach Resort, in Accra. Not in the hotel pool – no employees were allowed in the pool. No, she learned by struggling through the rough grey sea, on the other side of the resort walls. Rising and sinking, rising and sinking, on the dirty foam. No tourist ever stepped on to the beach (it was covered with trash), much less into the cold and treacherous sea. Nor did any of the other chambermaids. Only some reckless teenage boys, late at night, and Fatou, early in the morning. There is almost no way to compare swimming at Carib

Beach and swimming in the health centre, warm as it is, tranquil as a bath. And, as Fatou passes the Embassy of Cambodia, on her way to the pool, over the high wall she sees a shuttlecock, passed back and forth between two unseen players. The shuttlecock floats in a wide arc softly rightwards, and is smashed back, and this happens again and again, the first player always somehow able to retrieve the smash and transform it, once more, into a gentle, floating arc. High above, the sun tries to force its way through a cloud ceiling, grey and filled with water. Pock, smash. Pock, smash.

0—3

When the Embassy of Cambodia first appeared in our midst, a few years ago, some of us said, 'Well, if we were poets perhaps we could have written some sort of an ode about this surprising appearance of the embassy.' (For embassies are usually to be found in the centre of the city. This was the first one we had seen in the suburbs.) But we are not really a poetic people. We are from Willesden. Our minds tend towards the prosaic. I doubt there is a man or woman among us, for example, who – upon passing the Embassy of Cambodia for the first time – did not immediately think: 'genocide'.

O—4

Pock, smash. Pock, smash. This summer we watched the Olympics, becoming well attuned to grunting, and to the many other human sounds associated with effort and the triumph of the will. But the players in the garden of the Embassy of Cambodia are silent. (We can't say for sure that it is a garden – we have a limited view over the wall. It may well be a paved area, reserved for badminton.) The only sign that a game of badminton is under way at all is the motion of the shuttlecock itself, alternately being lobbed and smashed, lobbed and smashed, and always at the hour that Fatou passes on her way to the health centre to swim (just after ten in the morning on Mondays). It should be explained that it is Fatou's employers – and not Fatou – who are the true members of this health club; they have no idea she uses their guest passes in this way. (Mr and Mrs Derawal and their three children – aged seventeen, fifteen and ten – live on the same street as the embassy, but the road is almost a mile long, with the embassy at one end and the Derawals at the other.) Fatou's deception is possible only because on Mondays Mr Derawal drives to Eltham to visit his mini-market there, and Mrs Derawal works the counter in the family's second mini-mart, in Kensal Rise. In the slim drawer of a faux-Louis XVI console, in the entrance hall of the Derawals' primary residence, one can find a stockpile of guest passes. Nobody besides Fatou seems to remember that they are there.

Since 6 August (the first occasion on which she noticed the badminton), Fatou has made a point of pausing by the bus stop opposite the embassy for five or ten minutes before she goes in to swim, idle minutes she can hardly afford (Mrs Derawal returns to the house at lunchtime) and yet seems unable to forgo. Such is the strangely compelling aura of the embassy. Usually, Fatou gains nothing from this waiting and observing, but on a few occasions she has seen people arrive at the embassy and watched as they are buzzed through the gate. Young white people carrying rucksacks. Often they are scruffy, and wearing sandals, despite the cool weather. None of the visitors so far have been visibly Cambodian. These young people are likely looking for visas. They are buzzed in and then pass through the gate, although Fatou would really have to stand on top of the bus stop to get a view of whoever it is that lets them in. What she can say with certainty is that these occasional arrivals have absolutely no effect on the badminton, which continues in its steady pattern, first gentle, then fast, first soft and high, then hard and low.

0—5

On 20 August, long after the Olympians had returned to their respective countries, Fatou noticed that a basketball hoop had appeared in the far corner of the garden, its net of synthetic white rope rising high enough to be seen over the wall. But no basketball was ever played – at least not when Fatou was passing. The following week it had been moved closer to Fatou's side of the wall. (It must be a mobile hoop, on casters.) Fatou waited a week, two weeks, but still no basketball game replaced the badminton, which carried on as before.

o—6

When I say that we were surprised by the appearance of the Embassy of Cambodia, I don't mean to suggest that the embassy is in any way unique in its peculiarity. In fact, this long, wide street is notable for a number of curious buildings, in the context of which the Embassy of Cambodia does not seem especially strange. There is a mansion called GARYLAND, with something else in Arabic engraved below GARYLAND, and both the English and the Arabic text are inlaid in pink-and-green marble pillars that bookend a gigantic fence, far higher than the embassy's, better suited to a fortress. Dramatic golden gates open automatically to let vehicles in and out. At any one time, GARYLAND has five to seven cars parked in its driveway.

There is a house with a huge pink elephant on the doorstep, apparently made of mosaic tiles.

There is a Catholic nunnery with a single red Ford Focus parked in front. There is a Sikh institute. There is a faux-Tudor house with a pool that Mickey Rooney rented for a season, while he was performing in the West End fifteen summers ago. That house sits opposite a dingy retirement home, where one sometimes sees distressed souls, barely covered by their dressing gowns, standing on their tiny balconies, staring into the tops of the chestnut trees.

So we are hardly strangers to curious

buildings, here in Willesden and Brondesbury. And yet still we find the Embassy of Cambodia a little surprising. It is not the right sort of surprise, somehow.

O—7

In a discarded *Metro* found on the floor of the Derawal kitchen, Fatou read with interest a story about a Sudanese 'slave' living in a rich man's house in London. It was not the first time that Fatou had wondered if she herself was a slave, but this story, brief as it was, confirmed in her own mind that she was not. After all, it was her father, and not a kidnapper, who had taken her from Ivory Coast to Ghana, and when they reached Accra they had both found employment in the same hotel. Two years later, when she was eighteen, it was her father again who had organized her difficult passage to Libya and then on to Italy – a not insignificant financial sacrifice on his part. Also, Fatou could read English – and speak a little Italian – and this girl in the paper could not read or speak anything except the language of her tribe. And nobody beat Fatou, although Mrs Derawal had twice slapped her in the face, and the two older children spoke to her with no respect at all and thanked her for nothing. (Sometimes she heard her name used as a term of abuse between them. 'You're as black as Fatou.' Or 'You're as stupid as Fatou.') On the other hand, just like the girl in the newspaper, she had not seen her passport with her own eyes since she arrived at the Derawals', and she had been told from the start that her wages were to be retained by the Derawals to pay for the food and water and heat she would require during her stay, as well as to cover the rent for the room she slept in.

In the final analysis, however, Fatou was not confined to the house. She had an Oyster Card, given to her by the Derawals, and was trusted to do the food shopping and other outside tasks, for which she was given cash and told to return with change and receipts for everything. If she did not go out in the evenings that was only because she had no money with which to go out, and anyway knew very few people in London. Whereas the girl in the paper was not allowed to leave her employers' premises, not ever — she was a prisoner.

On Sunday mornings, for example, Fatou regularly left the house, to meet her church friend Andrew Okonkwo at the 98 bus stop and go with him to worship at the Sacred Heart of Jesus, just off the Kilburn High Road. Afterwards Andrew always took her to a Tunisian café, where they had coffee and cake, which Andrew, who worked as a night guard in the City, always paid for. And on Mondays Fatou swam. In very warm water, and thankful for the semi-darkness in which the health club, for some reason, kept its clientele, as if the place were a nightclub, or a midnight Mass. The darkness helped disguise the fact that her swimming costume was in fact a sturdy black bra and a pair of plain black cotton knickers. No, on balance she did not think she was a slave.

0—8

The woman exiting the Embassy of Cambodia did not look especially like a New Person or an Old Person – neither clearly of the city nor the country – and of course it is a long time since this division meant anything in Cambodia. Nor did these terms mean anything to Fatou, who was curious only to catch her first sighting of a possible Cambodian anywhere near the Embassy of Cambodia. She was particularly interested in the woman's clothes, which were precise and utilitarian – a grey shirt tucked tightly into a pair of tan slacks, a blue mackintosh, a droopy rain hat – just as if she were a man, or no different from a man. Her straight black hair was cut short. She had in her hands many bags from Sainsbury's, and this Fatou found a little mysterious: where was she taking all that shopping? It also surprised her that the woman from the Embassy of Cambodia should shop in the same Willesden branch of Sainsbury's where Fatou shopped for the Derawals. She had an idea that Oriental people had their own, secret establishments and shopped there. (She believed the Jews did, too.) She both admired and slightly resented this self-reliance, but had no doubt that it was the secret to holding great power, as a people. For example, when the Chinese had come to Fatou's village to take over the mine, an abiding local mystery had been: what did they eat and where did they eat it? They certainly did not buy food in the market, or from the Lebanese traders along the main road.

They made their own arrangements. (Whether back home or here, the key to surviving as a people, in Fatou's opinion, was to make your own arrangements.)

But, looking again at the bags the Cambodian woman carried, Fatou wondered whether they weren't in fact very old bags – hadn't their design changed? The more she looked at them the more convinced she became that they contained not food but clothes or something else again, the outline of each bag being a little too rounded and smooth. Maybe she was simply taking out the rubbish. Fatou stood at the bus stop and watched until the Cambodian woman reached the corner, crossed and turned left towards the high road. Meanwhile, back at the embassy the badminton continued to be played, though with a little more effort now because of a wayward wind. At one point it seemed to Fatou that the next lob would blow southwards, sending the shuttlecock over the wall to land lightly in her own hands. Instead the other player, with his vicious reliability (Fatou had long ago decided that both players were men), caught the shuttlecock as it began to drift and sent it back to his opponent – another deathly, downward smash.

0—9

No doubt there are those who will be critical of the narrow, essentially local scope of Fatou's interest in the Cambodian woman from the Embassy of Cambodia, but we, the people of Willesden, have some sympathy with her attitude. The fact is if we followed the history of every little country in this world – in its dramatic as well as its quiet times – we would have no space left in which to live our own lives or to apply ourselves to our necessary tasks, never mind indulge in occasional pleasures, like swimming.

Surely there is something to be said for drawing a circle around our attention and remaining within that circle. But how large should this circle be?

O—IO

It was the Sunday after Fatou saw the Cambodian that she decided to put a version of this question to Andrew, as they sat in the Tunisian café eating two large fingers of dough stuffed with cream and custard and topped with a strip of chocolate icing. Specifically, she began a conversation with Andrew about the Holocaust, as Andrew was the only person she had found in London with whom she could have these deep conversations, partly because he was patient and sympathetic to her, but also because he was an educated person, presently studying for a part-time business degree at the College of North West London. With his student card he had been given free, twenty-four-hour access to the Internet.

'But more people died in Rwanda,' Fatou argued. 'And nobody speaks about that! Nobody!'

'Yes, I think that's true,' Andrew conceded, and put the first of four sugars in his coffee. 'I have to check. But, yes, millions and millions. They hide the true numbers, but you can see them online. There's always a lot of hiding; it's the same all over. It's like this bureaucratic Nigerian government – they are the greatest at numerology, hiding figures, changing them to suit their purposes. I have a name for it: I call it "demonology". Not "numerology" – "demonology".'

'Yes, but what I am saying is like this,' Fatou pressed, wary of the conversation's drifting back, as it usually did, to the financial corruption of the Nigerian government. 'Are we born to suffer?

Sometimes I think we were born to suffer more than all the rest.'

Andrew pushed his professorial glasses up his nose. 'But, Fatou, you're forgetting the most important thing. Who cried most for Jesus? His mother. Who cries most for you? Your father. It's very logical, when you break it down. The Jews cry for the Jews. The Russians cry for the Russians. We cry for Africa, because we are Africans, and, even then, I'm sorry, Fatou' – Andrew's chubby face creased up in a smile – 'if Nigeria plays Ivory Coast and we beat you into the ground, I'm laughing, man! I can't lie. I'm celebrating. Stomp! Stomp!'

He did a little dance with his upper body, and Fatou tried, not for the first time, to imagine what he might be like as a husband, but could see only herself as the wife, and Andrew as a teenage son of hers, bright and helpful, to be sure, but a

27

son all the same – though in reality he was three years older than she. Surely it was wrong to find his baby fat and struggling moustache so off-putting. Here was a good man! She knew that he cared for her, was clean and had given his life to Christ. Still, some part of her rebelled against him, some unholy part.

'Hush your mouth,' she said, trying to sound more playful than disgusted, and was relieved when he stopped jiggling and laid both his hands on the table, his face suddenly quite solemn.

'Believe me, that's a natural law, Fatou, pure and simple. Only God cries for us all, because we are *all* his children. It's very, very logical. You just have to think about it for a moment.'

Fatou sighed, and spooned some coffee foam into her mouth. 'But I still think we have more pain. I've seen it myself. Chinese people have never been slaves. They are always protected from the worst.'

Andrew took off his glasses and rubbed them on the end of his shirt. Fatou could tell that he was preparing to lay knowledge upon her.

'Fatou, think about it for a moment, please: what about Hiroshima?'

It was a name Fatou had heard before, but sometimes Andrew's superior knowledge made her nervous. She would find herself struggling to remember even the things she had believed she already knew.

'The big wave . . .' she began, uncertainly – it was the wrong answer. He laughed mightily and shook his head at her.

'No, man! Big bomb. Biggest bomb in the world, made by the USA, of course. They killed five million people in *one second*. Can you imagine that? You think just because your eyes are like this' – he tugged the skin at both temples – 'you're always protected? Think again. This bomb, even if it didn't blow you up, a week later it melted the skin off your bones.'

Fatou realized she had heard this story before, or some version of it. But she felt the same vague impatience with it as she did with all accounts of suffering in the distant past. For what could be done about the suffering of the distant past?

'OK,' she said. 'Maybe all people have their hard times, in the past of history, but I still say –'

'Here is a counterpoint,' Andrew said, reaching out and gripping her shoulder. 'Let me ask you, Fatou, seriously, think about this. I'm sorry to interrupt you, but I have thought a lot about this and I want to pass it on to you, because I know you care about things seriously, not like these people –' He waved a hand at the assortment of cake eaters at other tables. 'You're not like the other girls I know, just thinking about the club and their hair. You're a person who thinks. I told you before, anything you want to know about, ask me – I'll look it up, I'll do the research. I have access. Then I'll bring it to you.'

'You're a very good friend to me, Andrew, I know that.'

'Listen, we are friends to each other. In this world you need friends. But, Fatou, listen to my question. It's a counterpoint to what you have been saying. Tell me, why would God choose us especially for suffering when we, above all others, praise his name? Africa is the fastest-growing Christian continent! Just think about it for a minute! It doesn't even make sense!'

'But it's not him,' Fatou said quietly, looking over Andrew's shoulder to the rain beating on the window. 'It's the Devil.'

O—II

Andrew and Fatou sat in the Tunisian coffee shop, waiting for it to stop raining, but it did not stop raining and at three p.m. Fatou said she would just have to get wet. She shared Andrew's umbrella as far as the Overground, letting him pull her into his clammy, high-smelling body as they walked. At Brondesbury station Andrew had to get the train, and so they said goodbye. Several times he tried to press his umbrella on her, but Fatou knew the walk from Acton Central to Andrew's bedsit was long and she refused to let him suffer on her account.

'Big woman. Won't let anybody protect you.'

'Rain doesn't scare me.'

Fatou took from her pocket a swimming cap she had found on the floor of the health club changing room. She wound her plaits into a bun and pulled the cap over her head.

'That's a very original idea,' Andrew said, laughing. 'You should market that! Make your first million!'

'Peace be with you,' Fatou said, and kissed him chastely on the cheek.

Andrew did the same, lingering a little longer with his kiss than was necessary.

O—12

By the time Fatou reached the Derawals' only her hair was dry, but before going to get changed she rushed to the kitchen to take the lamb out of the freezer, though it was pointless – there were not enough hours before dinner – and then upstairs to collect the dirty clothes from the matching wicker baskets in four different bedrooms. There was no one in the master bedroom, or in Faizul's or Julie's. Downstairs a television was blaring. Entering Asma's room, hearing nothing, assuming it empty, Fatou headed straight for the laundry basket in the corner. As she opened the lid she felt a hand hit her hard on the back; she turned around.

There was the youngest, Asma, in front of her, her mouth open like a trout fish. Before Fatou could understand, Asma punched the huge pile of clothes out of her hands. Fatou stooped to retrieve them. While she was kneeling on the floor, another strike came, a kick to her arm. She left the clothes where they were and got up, frightened by her own anger. But when she looked at Asma now she saw the girl gesturing frantically at her own throat, then putting her hands together in prayer and then back to her throat once more. Her eyes were bulging. She veered suddenly to the right; she threw herself over the back of a chair. When she turned back to Fatou her face was grey and Fatou understood finally and ran to her, grabbed her round her waist and pulled upwards as she had been taught in the hotel.

A marble – with an iridescent ribbon of blue at its centre, like a wave – flew from the child's mouth and landed wetly in the carpet's plush.

Asma wept and drew in frantic gulps of air. Fatou gave her a hug, and worried when the clothes would get done. Together they went down to the den, where the rest of the family was watching *Britain's Got Talent* on a flat-screen TV attached to the wall. Everybody stood at the sight of Asma's wild weeping. Mr Derawal paused the Sky box. Fatou explained about the marble.

'How many times I tell you not to put things in your mouth?' Mr Derawal asked, and Mrs Derawal said something in their language – Fatou heard the name of their God – and pulled Asma on to the sofa and stroked her daughter's silky black hair.

'I couldn't breathe, man! I couldn't call nobody,' Asma cried. 'I was gonna die!'

'What you putting marbles in your mouth for anyway, you idiot?' Faizul said, and unpaused the Sky box. 'What kind of chief puts a marble in her mouth? Idiot. Bet you was bricking it.'

'Oi, she saved your life,' said Julie, the eldest child, whom Fatou generally liked the least. 'Fatou saved your life. That's deep.'

'I woulda just done this,' Faizul said, and performed an especially dramatic Heimlich to his own skinny body. 'And if that didn't work I woulda just start pounding myself karate style, bam bam bam bam bam –'

'Faizul!' Mr Derawal shouted, and then turned stiffly to Fatou, and spoke not to her, exactly, but to a point somewhere between her elbow and the sunburst mirror behind her head. 'Thank you, Fatou. It's lucky you were there.'

Fatou nodded and went to leave, but at the doorway to the den Mrs Derawal asked her if the

37

lamb had defrosted and Fatou had to confess that she had only just taken it out. Mrs Derawal said something sharply in her language. Fatou waited for something further, but Mr Derawal only smiled awkwardly at her, and nodded as a sign that she could go now. Fatou went upstairs to collect the clothes.

0—13

'To keep you is no benefit. To destroy you is no loss' was one of the mottoes of the Khmer Rouge. It referred to the New People, those city dwellers who could not be made to give up city life and work on a farm. By returning everybody back to the land, the regime hoped to create a society of Old People – that is to say, of agrarian peasants. When a New Person was relocated from the city to the country, it was vital not to show weakness in the fields. Vulnerability was punishable by death.

In Willesden, we are almost all New People,

though some of us, like Fatou, were, until quite recently, Old People, working the land in our various countries of origin. Of the Old and New People of Willesden I speak; I have been chosen to speak for them, though they did not choose me and must wonder what gives me the right. I could say, 'Because I was born at the crossroads of Willesden, Kilburn and Queen's Park!' But the reply would be swift and damning: 'Oh, don't be foolish, many people were born right there; it doesn't mean anything at all. We are not one people and no one can speak for us. It's all a lot of nonsense. We see you standing on the balcony, overlooking the Embassy of Cambodia, in your dressing gown, staring into the chestnut trees, looking gormless. The real reason you speak in this way is because you can't think of anything better to do.'

O—14

On Monday, Fatou went swimming. She paused to watch the badminton. She thought that the arm that delivered the smashes must make a movement similar to the one she made in the pool, with her clumsy yet effective front crawl. She entered the health centre and gave a guest pass to the girl behind the desk. In the dimly lit changing room, she put on her sturdy black underwear. As she swam, she thought of Carib Beach. Her father serving snapper to the guests on the deck, his bow tie always a little askew, the ugly tourists, the whole scene there. Of course, it was not surprising in the least to see old white men from Germany with beautiful local girls on their laps, but she would never forget the two old white women from England – red women, really, thanks to the sun – each of them as big as two women put together, with Kweku and Osai lying by their sides, the boys hooking their scrawny black bird-arms round the women's massive red shoulders, and dancing with them in the hotel 'ballroom', answering to the names Michael and David, and disappearing into the women's cabins at night. She had known the boys' real girlfriends; they were chambermaids like Fatou. Sometimes they cleaned the rooms where Kweku and Osai spent the night with the English women. And the girls themselves had 'boyfriends' among the guests. It was not a holy place, that hotel. And the pool was shaped like a kidney bean: nobody could really swim in it, or showed any sign of wanting to.

Mostly, they stood in it and drank cocktails. Sometimes they even had their burgers delivered to the pool. Fatou hated to watch her father crouching to hand a burger to a man waist-high in water.

The only good thing that happened in Carib Beach was this: once a month, on a Sunday, the congregation of a local church poured out of a coach at the front gates, lined up fully dressed in the courtyard and then walked into the pool for a mass baptism. The tourists were never warned, and Fatou never understood why the congregants were allowed to do it. But she loved to watch their white shirts bloat and spread across the surface of the water, and to hear the weeping and singing. At the time – though she was not then a member of that church, or of any church except the one in her heart – she had felt that this baptism was for her, too, and that it kept her safe, and that this was somehow the reason she did not become one of the 'girls' at the Carib Beach Resort. In almost two years – between her father's efforts and the grace of an unseen and unacknowledged God – she did her work, and swam Sunday mornings at the crack of dawn, and got along all right. But the Devil was waiting.

She had only a month left in Accra when she entered a bedroom to clean it one morning and heard the door shut softly behind her before she could put a hand to it. He came, this time, in Russian form. Afterwards, he cried and begged her not to tell anyone: his wife had gone to see the Cape Coast Castle and they were leaving the following morning. Fatou listened to his blub-bering and realized that he thought the hotel would punish him for his action, or that the police would be called. That was when she knew that the Devil was stupid as well as evil. She spat in his face and left. Thinking about the Devil now made her swimming fast and angry, and for a while she easily lapped the young white man in the lane next to hers, the faster lane.

O—15

'Don't give the Devil your anger, it is his food,'
Andrew said to her, when they first met, a year
ago. He handed her a leaflet as she sat eating a
sandwich on a bench in Kilburn Park. 'Don't
make it so easy for him.' Without being invited,
he took the seat next to hers and began going
through the text of his leaflet. It was printed to
look like a newspaper, and he started with the
headline: 'WHY IS THERE PAIN?' She liked
him. They began a theological conversation. It
continued in the Tunisian café, and every Sunday
for several months. A lot of the things he said she

had heard before from other people, and they did not succeed in changing her attitude. In the end, it was one thing that he said to her that really made the difference. It was after she'd told him this story:

'One day, at the hotel, I heard a commotion on the beach. It was early morning. I went out and I saw nine children washed up dead on the beach. Ten or eleven years old, boys and girls. They had gone into the water, but they didn't know how to swim. Some people were crying, maybe two people. Everyone else just shook their heads and carried on walking to where they were going. After a long time, the police came. The bodies were taken away. People said, "Well, they are with God now." Everybody carried on like before. I went back to work. The next year I was in Rome. I saw a boy who was about fifteen years old knocked down on his bike. He was dead.

People were screaming and crying in the street. Everybody crying. They were not his family. They were only strangers. The next day, it was in the paper.'

And Andrew replied, 'A tap runs fast the first time you switch it on.'

O—16

Twenty more laps. Fatou tried to think of the last time she had cried. It was in Rome, but it wasn't for the boy on the bike. She was cleaning toilets in a Catholic girls' school. She did not know Jesus then, so it made no difference what kind of school it was – she only knew she was cleaning toilets. At midday, she had a fifteen-minute break. She would go to the little walled garden across the road to smoke a cigarette. One day, she was sitting on a bench near a fountain and spotted something odd in the bushes. A tin of green paint. A gold spray can. A Statue of Liberty costume. An identity card with the name Rajib Devanga. One shoe. An empty wallet. A plastic tub with a slit cut in the top meant for coins and euro notes – empty. A little stain of what looked like blood on this tub. Until that point, she had been envious of the Bengali boys on Via Nazionale. She felt that she, too, could paint herself green and stand still for an hour. But when she tried to find out more the Bengalis would not talk to her. It was a closed shop, for brown men only. Her place was in the toilet stalls. She thought those men had it easy. Then she saw that little sad pile of belongings in the bush and cried; for herself or for Rajib, she wasn't sure.

Now she turned on to her back in the water for the final two laps, relaxed her arms and kicked her feet out like a frog. Water made her think of more water. 'When you're baptized in our church, all sin is wiped, you start again': Andrew's promise. She had never told Andrew of the sin precisely, but she knew that he knew she was not a virgin. The day she finally became a Catholic, 6 February 2011, Andrew had taken her, hair still wet, to the Tunisian café and asked her how it felt.

She was joyful! She said, 'I feel like a new person!'

But happiness like that is hard to hold on to. Back at work the next day, picking Julie's dirty underwear up off the floor inches from the wicker basket, she had to keep reminding herself of her new relationship with Jesus and how it changed everything. Didn't it change everything? The following Sunday she expressed some of her doubt, cautiously, to Andrew.

'But did you think you'd never feel sad again? Never angry or tired or just pissed off — sorry about my language. Come on, Fatou! Wise up, man!'

Was it wrong to hope to be happy?

O—17

Lost to these watery thoughts, Fatou got home a little later than usual and was through the door only minutes before Mrs Derawal.

'How is Asma?' Fatou asked. She had heard the girl cry out in the night.

'My goodness, it was just a little marble,' Mrs Derawal said, and Fatou realized that it was not in her imagination: since Sunday night, neither of the adult Derawals had been able to look her in the eye. 'What a fuss everybody is making. I have a list for you – it's on the table.'

O—18

Fatou watched Andrew pick his way through the tables in the Tunisian café, holding a tray with a pair of mochas on it and some croissants. He hit the elbow of one man with his backside and then trailed the belt of his long, silly leather coat through the lunch of another, apologizing as he went. You could not say he was an elegant man. But he was generous, he was thoughtful. She stood up to push a teetering croissant back on to its plate. They sat down at the same time, and smiled at each other.

'A while ago you asked me about Cambodia,' Andrew said. 'Well, it's a very interesting case.'

He tapped the frame of his glasses. 'If you even wore a pair of these? They would kill you. Glasses meant you thought too much. They had very primitive ideas. They were enemies of logic and progress. They wanted everybody to go back to the country and live like simple people.'

'But sometimes it's true that things are simpler in the country.'

'In some ways. I don't really know. I've never lived in the country.'

I don't really know. It was good to hear him say that! It was a good sign. She smiled cheekily at him. 'People are less sinful in the country,' she said, but he did not seem to see she was flirting with him, and began upon another lecture.

'That's true. But you can't force people to live in the country. That's what I call a Big Man Policy. I invented this phrase for my dissertation. We know all about Big Man Policies in Nigeria.

They come from the top and they crush you. There's always somebody who wants to be the Big Man, and take everything for themselves, and tell everybody how to think and what to do. When, actually, it's he who is weak. But if the Big Men see that *you* see that *they* are weak they have no choice but to destroy you. That is the real tragedy.'

Fatou sighed. 'I never met a man who didn't want to tell everybody how to think and what to do,' she said.

Andrew laughed. 'Fatou, you include me? Are you a feminist now, too?'

Fatou brought her mug up to her lips and looked penetratingly at Andrew. There were good and bad kinds of weakness in men, and she had come to the conclusion that the key was to know which kind you were dealing with.

'Andrew,' she said, putting her hand on his, 'would you like to come swimming with me?'

O—19

Because Fatou believed that the Derawals' neighbours had been instructed to spy on her, she would not let Andrew come to the house to pick her up on Monday, instead leaving as she always did, just before ten, carrying misleading Sainsbury's bags and walking towards the health centre. She spotted him from a long way off – the road was so straight and he had arrived early. He stood shivering in the drizzle. She felt sorry, but also a little prideful: it was the prospect of seeing her body that had raised this big man from his bed. Still, it was a sacrifice, she knew, for her friend to come out to meet her on a weekday morning. He worked all night long and kept the daytime for sleeping. She watched him waving at her from their agreed meeting spot, just on the corner, in front of the Embassy of Cambodia. After a while, he stopped waving – because she was still so far away – and then, a little later, he began waving again. She waved back, and when she finally reached him they surprised each other by holding hands. 'I'm an excellent badminton player,' Andrew said, as they passed the Embassy of Cambodia. 'I would make you weep for mercy! Next time, instead of swimming we should play badminton somewhere.' Next time, we should go to Paris. Next time, we should go to the moon. He was a dreamer. But there are worse things, Fatou thought, than being a dreamer.

O—2O

'So you're a guest and this is your guest?' the girl behind the desk asked.

'I am a guest and this is another guest,' Fatou replied.

'Yeah . . . that's not really how it works?'

'Please,' Fatou said. 'We've come from a long way.'

'I appreciate that,' the girl said. 'But I really shouldn't let you in, to be honest.'

'Please,' Fatou said again. She could think of no other argument.

The girl took out a pen and made a mark on Fatou's guest pass.

'This one time. Don't tell no one I did this, please. One time only! I'll need to cross off two separate visits.'

For one time only, then, Andrew and Fatou approached the changing rooms together and parted at the doors that led to the men's and the women's. In her changing room, Fatou got ready with lightning speed. Yet somehow he was already there on a lounger when she came out, eyes trained on the women's changing-room door, waiting for her to emerge.

'Man, this is the life!' he said, putting his arms behind his head.

'Are you getting in?' Fatou asked, and tried to place her hands, casually, in front of her groin.

'Not yet, man, I'm just taking it all in, taking it all in. You go in. I'll come in a moment.'

Fatou climbed down the steps and began to swim. Not elegant, not especially fast, but consistent and determined. Every now and then she would angle her head to try to see if Andrew was still on his chair, smiling to himself. After twenty laps, she swam to where he lay and put her elbows on the tiles.

'You're not coming in? It's so warm. Like a bath.'

'Sure, sure,' he said. 'I'll try it.'

As he sat up his stomach folded in on itself, and Fatou wondered whether he had spent all that time on the lounger to avoid her seeing its precise bulk and wobble. He came towards the stairs; Fatou held out a hand to him, but he pushed it away. He made his way down and stood in the shallow end, splashing water over his shoulders like a prince fanning himself, and then crouching down into it.

'It is warm! Very nice. This is the life, man! You go, swim – I'll follow you.'

Fatou kicked off, creating so much splash she heard someone in the adjacent lane complain. At the wall, she turned and looked for Andrew. His method, such as it was, involved dipping deep under the water and hanging there like a hippo, then batting his arms till he crested for air, and then diving down again and hanging. It was a lot of energy to expend on a short distance, and by the time he reached the wall he was panting like a maniac. His eyes – he had no goggles – were painfully red.

'It's OK,' Fatou said, trying to take his hand again. 'If you let me, I'll show you how.' But he shrugged her off and rubbed at his eyes.

'There's too much bloody chlorine in this pool.'

'You want to leave?'

Andrew turned back to look at Fatou. His eyes were streaming. He looked, to Fatou, like a little boy trying to disguise the fact he had been crying. But then he held her hand, under the water.

'No. I'm just going to take it easy right here.'

'OK,' Fatou said.

'You swim. You're good. You swim.'

'OK,' Fatou said, and set off, and she found that each lap was more distracted and rhythmless than the last. She was not used to being watched while she swam. Ten laps later, she suddenly stood up halfway down the lane and walked the rest of the distance to the wall.

'You want to go in the Jacuzzi?' she asked him, pointing to it.

In the hot tub sat a woman dressed in a

soaking tracksuit, her head covered with a headscarf. A man next to the woman, perhaps her husband, stared at Fatou and said something to the woman. He was so hairy he was almost as covered as she was. Together they rose up out of the water and left. He was wearing the tiniest of Speedos, the kind Fatou had feared Andrew might wear, and was grateful he had not. Andrew's shorts were perfectly nice, knee-length, red and solid, and looked good against his skin.

'No,' Andrew said. 'It's great just to be here with you, watching the world go by.'

0—21

That same evening, Fatou was fired. Not for the guest passes – the Derawals never found out how many miles Fatou had travelled on their membership. In fact, it was hard for Fatou to understand exactly why she was being fired, as Mrs Derawal herself did not seem able to explain it very precisely.

'What you don't understand is that we have no need for a nanny,' she said, standing in the doorway of Fatou's room – there was not really enough space in there for two people to stand without one of them being practically on the bed.

'The children are grown. We need a housekeeper, one who cleans properly. These days, you care more about the children than the cleaning,' Mrs Derawal added, though Fatou had never cared for the children, not even slightly. 'And that is of no use to us.'

Fatou said nothing. She was thinking that she did not have a proper suitcase and would have to take her things from Mrs Derawal's house in plastic bags.

'And so you will want to find somewhere else to live as soon as possible,' Mrs Derawal said. 'My husband's cousin is coming to stay in this room on Friday – this Friday.'

Fatou thought about that for a moment. Then she said, 'Can I please use the phone for one call?'

Mrs Derawal inspected a piece of wood that had flaked from the doorframe. But she nodded.

'And I would like to have my passport, please.'

'Excuse me?'

'My passport, please.'

At last Mrs Derawal looked at Fatou, right into her eyes, but her face was twisted, as if Fatou had just reached over and slapped her. Anyone could see the Devil had climbed inside poor Mrs Derawal. He was lighting her up with a pure fury.

'For goodness' sake, girl, I don't have your passport! What would I want with your passport? It's probably in a drawer in the kitchen some-where. Is that my job now, too, to look for your things?'

Fatou was left alone. She packed her things into the decoy shopping bags she usually took to the swimming pool. While she was doing this, someone pushed her passport under her door. An hour later she carried her bags downstairs and went directly to the phone in the hall. Faizul walked by and lifted his hand for a high-five. Fatou ignored him and dialled Andrew's number. From her friend's voice she knew that she had woken him, but he was not even the slightest bit angry. He listened to all she had to say and seemed to understand, too, without her having to say so, that at this moment she could not speak freely. After she had said her part, he asked a few quick technical questions and then explained clearly and carefully what was to happen.

'It will all be OK. They need cleaners in my offices – I will ask for you. In the meantime, you come here. We'll sleep in shifts. You can trust me. I respect you, Fatou.'

But she did not have her Oyster Card; it was in the kitchen, on the fridge under a magnet of Florida, and she would rather die than go in there. Fine: he could meet her at six p.m. at Brondesbury Overground station. Fatou looked at the grandfather clock in front of her: she had four hours to kill.

'Six o'clock,' she repeated. She put the phone down, took the rest of the guest passes from the drawer of the faux-Louis XVI console and left the house.

'Weighed down a bit today,' the girl at the desk of the health club said, nodding at Fatou's collection of plastic bags. Fatou held out a guest pass for a stamp and did not smile. 'See you next time,' this same girl said, an hour and a half later, as Fatou strode past, still weighed down and still unwilling to be grateful for past favours. Gratitude was just another kind of servitude. Better to make your own arrangements.

Walking out into the cold grey, Fatou felt a sense of brightness, of being washed clean, that neither the weather nor her new circumstances could dim. Still, her limbs were weary and her hair was wet; she would probably catch a cold, waiting out here. It was only four thirty. She put her bags on the pavement and sat down next to them, just by the bus stop opposite the Embassy of Cambodia. Buses came and went, slowing down for her and then jerking forward when they realized that she had no interest in getting up and on. Many of us walked past her that afternoon, or spotted her as we rode the bus, or through the windscreens of our cars, or from our balconies. Naturally, we wondered what this girl was doing, sitting on the damp pavement in the middle of the day. We worried for her. We tend to assume the worst, here in Willesden. We watched her watching the shuttlecock. Pock, smash. Pock, smash. As if one player could imagine only a violent conclusion and the other only a hopeful return.